(Inside – About this story . . .)

This sweet story unfolds with a young girl, Brooke Lynn, feeling a warm connection with a ladybug she met briefly, and hopes to find this newfound friend again. Along the way, her mother shows her how to tenderly handle a ladybug, where they live and maybe just maybe bring some 'good luck'. Brooke Lynn's adventurous, yet hasty search, leads her to the final discovery... right in her backyard! *My Lil' Ladybug Friend* fills the heart throughout but especially as she says genuinely, "Til we meet again, my lil' friend, good luck...." – *Toby A. Williams*

Publishing Information & Credits

Toby A. Williams, Self-Published on December, 2018.

ISBN: 978-1-7917-0493-3

The BROOKE LYNN Adventures Series

Book #1 My Lil' Ladybug Friend, Released December 2018
Book #2 My Lil' Big Ocean, Releasing Summer 2019

This is a fictional children's story and not based on any actual persons, places or events (living or deceased). Any resemblance is entirely coincidental.

Illustrated by award-winning artist Corrina Holyoake

Edited by Toby A. Williams and Sue Campion

Dedication

This book is dedicated to my precious niece, Jessica Weber.
May she and her children remember to freely frolic
with the butterflies and ladybugs.

Gratitude of Thanks

A special thank you to my friend, poet and writer, Sue Campion. Sue not only taught me how to believe in my creative writing ability but she was an invaluable "second set of eyes" during the editing process. Her mentoring (and prodding) helped enlighten my imagination and thus, enhance my storytelling.

And most especially, a note of love and gratitude to my best friend and supportive husband, Duane Williams. Together, we have held hands during life's calamities and precious milestones. What an exciting ride!

With humble love – *Toby A. Williams*

Magical moments happen,

    during each and every day.

One such moment mystified me,

    in a most unusual way.

Hello there, friend — Brooke Lynn here,

    explorer of all things wild.

Join me as we discover,

    our untamed inner-most child.

Here's a story of one adventure,

    a snippet you're sure to survive.

If we only open our eyes and explore,

    these moments will come alive.

Today, we'll find a tiny small dot,

    that's red with a few black spots.

Come along carefully with me,

    as it jumps around lots and lots!

One delightful summer day,

    I jumped on my swing to play.

Something strange suddenly fell on me,

    from above, to my dismay.

Tumbling onto my shoulder,

    this dark spot landed so easily.

Do you see that small red dot?

    Well, it certainly startled me!

Jumping and squealing – oh my,

whatever should I do?

"Mom, what's this dot? Come quick!

Take a look, please and thank you!"

It sat on my arm, then crawled,

down to my hand, then disappeared!

I grew frightened and worried,

maybe, even a wee bit scared?!

Mom hurried toward me to see,

what was up with this red spot.

"Why, it's a sweet ladybug, dear Brooke,

and not just any ol' dot!"

"They're friendly and fun to watch.

I hear they're full of good luck.

Will it walk onto my hand?

Or, oops, hopelessly get stuck!"

She placed her hand on my arm,

softly, with barely a touch.

The spot moved onto her fingertip,

and began hopping way too much!

This dot with its stubby short legs,

wobbled over Mom's white knuckle.

Then onto her thumb it stopped,

causing us to laugh and to chuckle!

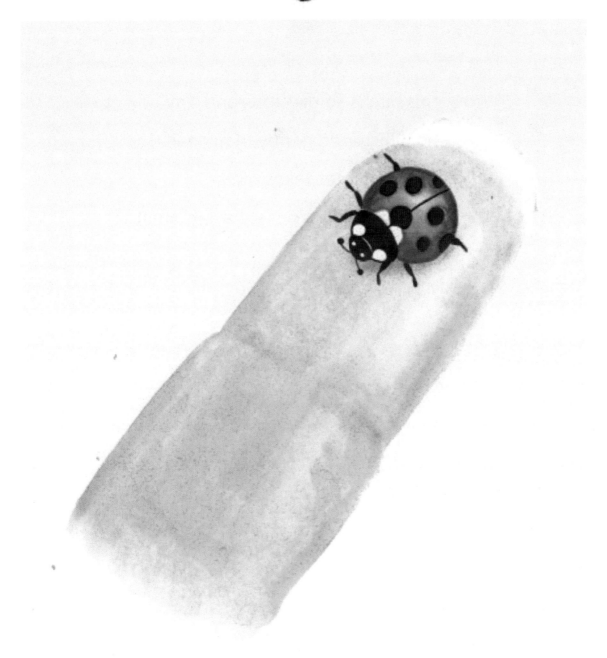

"Wow, this bug is so precious and tiny",

she whispered gently in my ear.

"Before this little dot takes off,

look carefully, Brooke, have no fear."

Lifting and stretching my neck,

to get a much closer view.

I saw more red than black on its back,

and six small skinny legs, too!

"Let's count this little one's spots,

quickly while it's still here.

We haven't much more time,

'til our freckly friend flies in the air."

"One, two, three and four, I see,

oh, Brooke, there's another one!

Five, six, and **seven**", we sang.

Together, it was so much fun!

"**Seven** dark spots! What's next Mom?"

I stood still as my mouth grew dry.

Then Mom said, "Brooke, make a wish,

say 'good luck', and a sweet 'goodbye'."

One more glance, oh dare I look?

The dot hopped as if to fly.

Mom slowly closed both her eyes,

to make a wish — and so did I!

When Mom opened her eyes,

    she sucked in a breath so deep.

Then Mom blew softly over this dot,

    with nary a sound, nor a peep.

The dot fluttered, it flitted – then flew,

    taking flight way up so high.

"Til we meet again, my lil' friend,

    good luck, Lil' Ladybug, bye-bye."

Night fall had come, time for bed,

I snuggled in tightly to stay.

With my favorite warm PJ's on,

tomorrow promised a new day.

Mom tucked me in bed so snug.

She giggled, then said, "Sleep tight!

Don't let the bed bugs bite!"

Then she kissed my cheek, "Good night."

A sneeze woke me up from sleep,

as I heard a thunderous yawn.

Then, a scuffling of Mom's slippered feet,

let me know it was finally dawn.

An excitement rose up in me,

to find my newfound friend.

Will you help me find this freckled speck?

Let's go, leave no loose ends!

Outside I cried, *"Now, don't give up!*
This is just another test.
I will find you, my Lil' Ladybug.
Until then, I won't rest!"

I searched with all my focus,
looking at each footprint I made.
Tip-toeing over the freshly mowed grass,
I watched for clues, blade-by-blade.

Trudging onward, I took a short pause,
next to our creaky old shed.
Should I give up this search, oh drats!
Or, is my ladybug just up ahead?

I ran past the tangled-up hose,

    where my feet made me stop, then drop.

Under the large lemon tree,

    at the edge of the lot, I plopped!

"Whew! I'm tired — need a break!"

    I cried with a long, winded sigh.

I stared up through the lemon limbs,

    as gray clouds darkened the sky.

My tummy started to gurgle,

    it must be about lunch time.

"Brooke Lynn, come on in and eat!"

    Mom hollered o'er the old wind chime.

Stepping on through the back door,

I glanced over at the side gate.

There's one place I've yet to explore,

after lunch, it'll have to wait!

My tummy was full after Mom's beef stew,

as my eyes drooped down a bit.

"It's nap time, Brooke Lynn," Mom said.

"Time to quit," I had to admit.

I woke up from a restful nap,

as a thought occurred to me.

I knew where to find Lil' Ladybug,

just exactly, where my friend would be!

This speckly dot will be in plain sight!

How simply simple I thought.

Why, in Mom's flower bed, right?

Resting on one of the garden pots!

Filled with loads of excitement,

    I scurried so fast – can't trip!

Almost forgot to tie my shoes,

    oops, be careful … almost a slip!

"Slow down, Brooke Lynn, what's the rush!

    There's plenty of time," Mom cried.

"Be in the backyard exploring,

    in the flower garden outside."

So many colorful flowers,

      each a different shape and size.

Would the freckled dot blend in?

      Or, leap like a big surprise?

I smelled the sweet fresh odor,

      of roses by the wooden fence.

Fragrance up my little nose,

      it was magical, and oh so dense.

A yellow-golden butterfly,

      waved its dotted wings nearby.

When something started to twitch,

      just barely catching my eye!

Slowly I walked past the garden gate,

to the middle of the patch.

And there I spied my spotted friend,

on a large flower where it latched.

My heart started to beat, thump-thump,

as I drew near inch-by-inch.

Carefully I approached the plant,

just hoping my friend wouldn't flinch!

My patience paid off, it's true.

It's hard to explain, you see.

Such a mystical magic moment,

happened right then and there to me!

And when I thought the spot would take off,

getting ready to fly away,

it just stopped ... and turned around.

Was my ladybug looking back my way?

The bug-a-boo's eyes were glassy and dark,

I could barely make them out.

Possibly, does ladybug see me?

But, of course, I have no doubt!

"Its home was here all along!"

I shouted into the flower bed.

Mom heard me and soon rushed out,

"Look, Mom, Lil' Ladybug's just ahead!"

A small cluster of ladybugs,

were gathered nearby standing tall.

How delightful! My Lil' Ladybug

was never alone after all!

And like my mother had shown me,

I tenderly stretched out my hand.

Then opened my palm really wide,

to offer it a safe place to land.

We stayed this way for a while,

    my hand serving as Ladybug's shelf.

Don't drop it, be very careful,

    I quietly thought to myself.

Then, with a strong hint of courage,

    and a gentle touch of love,

I was ready to let my friend go,

    fly far and soar high above.

With a flutter and a tiny step,

    its wings opened and soon spread.

Saying farewell's not so easy,

    I'd rather my friend stay instead!

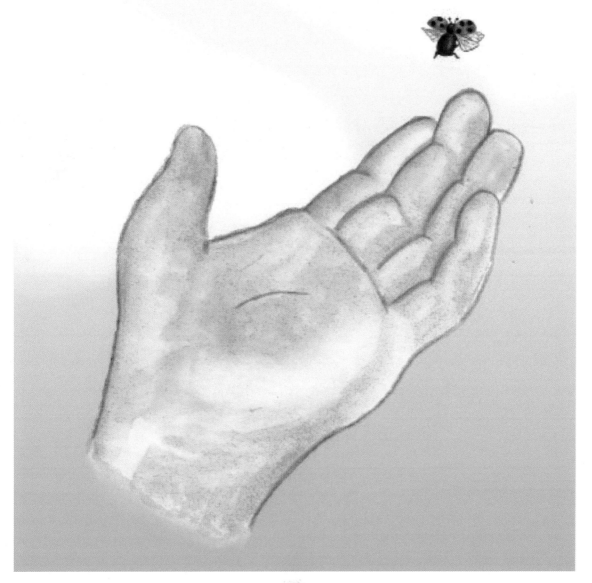

Quickly closing both my eyes,

    I thought of a whimsical wish.

It was a very magical moment,

    one I know I'll always cherish!

Blowing softly, Lil' Ladybug lifted,

    then climbed to a great new height.

"Good luck, my newfound friend.

    You've brought us so much delight."

Mom and I waved a hopeful 'so long',

    as the day turned into night.

"We needn't say a final good-bye.

    Maybe soon, we'll reunite."

The End

Factoids About Ladybugs

Ladybugs are called various names in different regions such as lady beetles, ladybug beetles, ladybird beetles to name just a few. There are usually 6-7 spots on each ladybug with 6 tiny thin legs (3 on each side to keep its balance). Most commonly, they have shiny red backs with black spots but in some regions, they may have an orange-rust coloring.

They eat mainly aphids in the garden which helps the plants grow and thrive. "Helpers" at heart in the garden, they are not considered a pest. Did you know ladybugs can live up to one year? In some colder climates, they will hibernate for the winter and wait for the warm Spring air to lay their eggs. And guess what? Ladybugs are not even a bug at all but from the beetle family! However, it is the Official State "Bug" of Massachusetts, New Hampshire, Delaware, Ohio, and Tennessee. Interesting, huh?

Ladybugs are considered good luck all over the world. One legend has it that a long time ago in Europe, farmers were feeling discouraged after many years of poor crops. They noticed something different one year — the crops were starting to do well. With a closer look, they realized their good fortune came from the presence of little beetle bugs on their plants. The tiny beetles were eating the pests on the plants. They felt their prayers had been answered. "Blessed Lady" (Virgin Mary) transformed into ladybug or lady beetles. After all, the Virgin Mary's cloak was red, and the seven black spots were seen as her Seven Sorrows. Whatever you may choose to believe, the ladybug offering of good wishes and good luck is universally practiced to this day.

About the Author

Toby A. Williams currently resides in the San Diego area of Southern California with her best friend, who also happens to be her dear husband. They enjoy travel, golf, helping out in the community and of course, reading and writing. Her inspiration to write children's stories was borne from her mother's childhood reflections *(Marianne Kilbourne Thompson, 1934-2013).*

Her mother fondly reminisced about a kind neighbor while growing up in New Hampshire. This woman had a magical name, Tasha Tudor *(1915-2008, American author & illustrator of children's literature).* Toby's mother spoke about the uniqueness Tasha Tudor had as a storyteller in capturing children's imaginations. "Look at the cow-cow-moo-caddities. That's what Tasha Tudor calls cows!", my mother would say with a smile.

Book Review

If you enjoyed this book, please consider leaving an honest review on Amazon or drop me a line at the e-mail address below. Your interest in children's literature and literacy is much appreciated. Thank you for coming along on this adventure.

Toby A. Williams, E-mail address: tawilms@outlook.com

You may also be interested in . . . the newest book in *The BROOK LYNN Adventures* series. Coming soon, *My Lil' Big Ocean*, Book #2. Brooke Lynn has never visited the ocean or seashore, and thus, her "first" trip to the coast promises to be larger than life for her! The contagious curiosity of a little girl, leads to an endless search for creatures along the shores. This story will have you and your child right along-side with Brooke Lynn as she scours for seashells. What treasures shall she find? — *Toby A. Williams*

Made in the USA
Middletown, DE
18 December 2019